The Storm

Anne Rockwell

ILLUSTRATED BY Robert Sauber

Hyperion Books for Children
New York

For Nicholas, Julianna, and Nigel
—A.R.

For the everlasting sunshine in my life, my wife
—R.S.

Text © 1994 by Anne Rockwell.
Illustrations © 1994 by Robert Sauber.
All rights reserved. Printed in the United States of America.
For information address Hyperion Books for Children,
114 Fifth Avenue, New York, New York 10011.

FIRST EDITION

1   3   5   7   9   10   8   6   4   2

Library of Congress Cataloging-in-Publication Data

Rockwell, Anne
The storm / by Anne Rockwell; illustrated by Robert Sauber — 1st ed.
p.   cm.
Summary: A girl and her family experience the power and excitement
of a big coastal storm.
ISBN 0-7868-0017-8 (trade) — ISBN 0-7868-2013-6 (lib. bdg.)
[1. Storms — Fiction.]   I. Sauber, Robert, ill.   II. Title.
PZ7.R5943Sr   1994   93-40976   CIP   AC
[E] — dc20

The artwork for each picture is prepared using gouache and colored pencil.
This book is set in 18-point Horley Old Style.

Autumn is when the big storms come.
They come fast, if they come at all.
That's what my mother says.
She knows, for she's always lived
in our house on the hill by the sea.

One day in October,
my mother and I walked home together.
The wind blew so hard it blew away the picture I made
and tore the red and yellow leaves from the trees.

In the village, we passed Mr. Fein.
He was rolling up the awning of his hardware store
and putting baskets and rakes inside.
"It's going to be a big one," he called.
"You'd better hurry home."

My father drives a bulldozer for our town.
Usually he's not home until long after we are.
But when we climbed the hill to our house,
he was already there,
putting trash cans and tools in the cellar.

"They let us off early," he said.
"But we'll have plenty to do tomorrow.
They say this storm is going to be a big one."

My father was right.
When we turned on the TV,
the announcer was talking about a very big storm
that was coming our way, fast.
She warned all the people who live down by the shore
to head for their local shelters.

Later, when I looked out the window,
I saw some of our neighbors
get into their cars and drive away.
An ambulance even came for Mrs. Hoff
because she was sick in bed.

We got ready, too.

My mother made sure our flashlight and radio had batteries.

My father found candles and matches and blankets.

I took down my bird feeder before it blew away.

While I was outside, Mr. Edwards came up the walk.

"I bought some extra bread and peanut butter

for you and your family," he said.

"Now hurry inside. I hear it's going to be a big one."

The moon was full that night,
but you couldn't find it hidden behind the clouds.
The wind blew harder.
Rain came down.
The tide came in so high, the sea covered the road.
A boat broke loose from its mooring
and crashed on the big rock at the bottom of our hill.

Then, out on the street, a tree branch broke off.
Suddenly the lights in our house flickered and went out.
"That branch must have knocked down the power lines,"
my father said, and helped me light the candles.

We couldn't cook supper, for the stove didn't work.
We ate peanut butter sandwiches by candlelight
and snuggled up together on the couch.
"We're very lucky," my mother said,
"to live up here, in our house on the hill."

All night long the wind blew and blew.
I could see trees bending,
and I heard loud cracks and crashes
when their branches fell.
Sirens wailed as fire engines came
to put out fires from fallen wires.

We didn't sleep much that night.
We kept looking out the window,
watching the wind and the rain and the waves.
"It ought to blow over soon," my father said.
But the storm kept on.

I must have fallen asleep at last,
because when I woke up, it was morning.

The storm had passed.
There was no more wind, and no more rain.
Even the sea had gone back where it belonged.

Orange trucks were bringing workers
to fix the wires the wind had knocked down.
Noisy chain saws were cutting up
the branches of fallen trees.
My father had gone to work very early,
before the sun was up.

After breakfast, my mother and I walked down the hill
to see what the storm had washed ashore.

Beach was where the road should have been.
Picnic tables were lying upside down and broken in the sand.
I saw tires and a door and an anchor without a boat.
I saw bottles and trash cans and ropes and lines
and pieces of wood and the roots of a tree,
all tangled together in seaweed.

Nothing was where it should have been.
Only the great blue heron was standing
in the cove where he always does.

A whole bed of mussels was washed ashore.
Seagulls were having a feast,
mewing and screaming as we hurried by.

"Hey there!" my father called
as his bulldozer pushed and shoved the sand
off the road and back to the beach.

I think everyone we know was walking
on the beach that morning.
My teacher was there with her little boy,
and Mr. Fein was there with his wife.

"Quite a mess, isn't it?" my mother said to Mr. Edwards.
"Yes," he said, "but at least no one was hurt."

Everyone was quiet as they looked at the clouds
and the shafts of sunlight shining.
The leftover wind smelled good.

That night, we saw the lights go on
in the houses down by the shore.

After supper, my father stretched and yawned.
"Haven't seen a storm like that since I was a kid," he said.
Then he climbed the stairs to bed
without even reading the paper.
"I guess it could have been worse," he said with a sigh.
"Sleep well," my mother said.
"We've got another big cleanup day tomorrow."

From my window I watched the bright round moon
shimmer and wobble in the calm black sea.
Storms come fast, if they come at all.
Then they are over and gone.